FLIP
and the
COWS

Also by Wesley Dennis

HOLIDAY

FLIP

FLIP AND THE MORNING

A CROW I KNOW

FLIP AND THE COWS

STORY AND PICTURES BY WESLEY DENNIS

NEW YORK · THE VIKING PRESS

FIRST PUBLISHED SEPTEMBER 1942

SECOND PRINTING AUGUST 1943

THIRD PRINTING JUNE 1944

FOURTH PRINTING JUNE 1945

FIFTH PRINTING AUGUST 1949

SIXTH PRINTING SEPTEMBER 1951

SEVENTH PRINTING JULY 1955

EIGHTH PRINTING MARCH 1959

LITHOGRAPHED IN U. S. A. BY REEHL LITHO COMPANY

PUBLISHED ON THE SAME DAY IN THE DOMINION OF CANADA BY

THE MACMILLAN COMPANY OF CANADA LIMITED

To Teddy Krautter

Flip was afraid of cows.

He didn't know just why—no cow had ever hurt
him or even tried to.

"But," Flip thought, "why do they have such sharp horns?

"Horns are not for smelling or eating—and they're no use for swishing flies," he said to himself.

"Guess they're meant for just one thing—to scare a colt like me."

But no matter how frightened he was, Flip liked
to hide behind the fences to watch the cows.

He would stare and stare, and then suddenly he would turn around and dash down to the other end of the field as far away as he could go.

One day he was so frightened that he dared not take his eyes from the cows long enough to turn around and run—so he started to back up. He backed as far as the brook and jumped it backward, still keeping his eyes on the cows.

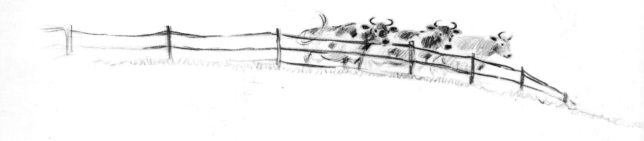

Flip had been jumping the brook backward a lot lately, because jumping it frontward had become so easy that it wasn't much fun any more.

Only this time he was so busy watching the cows
he didn't notice his mother on the other bank.

She was grazing near a thistle bush, and the first thing she knew her tender nose had been pushed right into it.

She didn't like this and she turned and nipped
Flip.

It didn't really hurt, but Flip thought it did. He forgot all about the cows and started to run as fast as he could.

MISSISSIPPI LIBRARY COMMISSION
405 State Office Building, Jackson

He didn't stop for fences or anything else, and soon he was farther from his mother than he ever had been before.

He only stopped then because he was out of breath.

He closed his eyes and was breathing hard and fast when he thought he heard a familiar sound —and it was very near.

At first Flip didn't dare open his eyes.

When he did, he opened one eye just a little. It was enough — he had run right into the field of cows!

Flip counted five staring at him. They all had long, sharp horns.

What could he do? Perhaps he could jump over
them and run away.

So he took a few steps backward to get a good
start.

But the cows were so curious to see Flip walking
backward that they crowded around still closer.

Flip was really scared now.

He backed up again in a rush and—

backed right into a sharp pair of horns.

"They've got me," screamed Flip, and jumped up so fast and so high that he just turned a somersault right in mid-air.

This was too much for the cows. They had never
seen anything like that.

As Flip came down he could see cows running
away in all directions.

Flip was astonished. "Horns or no horns," he said, "I'll never be afraid of cows again." And he never was.